# DOWN THE DRAIN!

# DOWN THE DRAIN!

## Robert Munsch          Michael Martchenko

SCHOLASTIC CANADA LTD.

New York  Toronto  London  Auckland  Sydney
Mexico City  New Delhi  Hong Kong  Buenos Aires

The illustrations in this book were painted in watercolour on Crescent illustration board.
The type is set in 21 point Dante.

Scholastic Canada Ltd.
604 King Street West, Toronto, Ontario M5V 1E1, Canada

Scholastic Inc.
557 Broadway, New York, NY 10012, USA

Scholastic Australia Pty Limited
PO Box 579, Gosford, NSW 2250, Australia

Scholastic New Zealand Limited
Private Bag 94407, Greenmount, Auckland, New Zealand

Scholastic Children's Books
Euston House, 24 Eversholt Street, London NW1 1DB, UK

Library and Archives Canada Cataloguing in Publication

Munsch, Robert N., 1945-
Down the drain! / Robert Munsch ; illustrations by Michael Martchenko.

ISBN 978-0-545-98600-7

I. Martchenko, Michael  II. Title.

PS8576.U575D69 2009          jC813'.54          C2008-905819-4

ISBN-10 0-545-98600-1

6  5  4  3  2          Printed in Canada          09  10  11

Mixed Sources
Cert no. SW-COC-001271
© 1996 FSC
FSC

The text has been printed on chlorine-free paper with 10% post-consumer waste.

*To Adam and Janna Lewis,*
*Guelph, Ontario*
*— R.M.*

Adam jumped HIGHER and HIGHER and **HIGHER** and **HIGHER** on the trampoline.

"That's too high," said his little sister. "You're gonna get in trouble!"

"Am not," said Adam.

"Are too," said his little sister.

"Am not," said Adam.

"Are too," said his little sister.

Then Adam clanged into one side of the trampoline, flew across the yard and landed in the large pile of ashes from last week's marshmallow fire.

"ADAM!" yelled his father. "Your hands are dirty. Your face is dirty. Your feet are dirty. Adam, you need a bath!"

"No, no, no!" said Adam.

"Soap in my eyes!

"Soap in my ears!

"Soap in my mouth!

"I do not like baths!"

Adam ran into the kitchen, grabbed the leg of the table and would not let go.

His little sister tickled his tummy. Adam laughed and laughed and let go of the table. His father picked him up, ran to the bathroom and dropped Adam in the bathtub, clothes and all.

Adam's dad turned on the water and the tub started to fill up.

*Blub* *Blub* **Blub** *Blub*

**Blub** *Blub*

Then the phone rang.

*Ring! Ring! Ring! Ring! Ring!*

"Stay right here, Adam," said his father. "Don't move. I'll be right back."

He ran down the hall, picked up the phone and said, "Hello? Hello? Hello? What's that? No money in the bank! But I can't talk right now, Adam is in the tub. Goodbye, goodbye, goodbye."

He hung up the phone, ran back to the bathroom, and was almost to the door when the phone rang again.

*Ring! Ring! Ring! Ring! Ring!*

He ran back down the
hall, picked up the phone and
said, "Hello? Hello? Hello? Grandma?
Sorry, I can't talk right now. Adam is in the
tub. Goodbye, goodbye, goodbye."

The phone rang again. He picked it up
and said, "Hello? Hello? Hello? NO! Adam can't
come and play. Adam is in the tub. Goodbye,
goodbye, goodbye."

When Adam's father finally got back to the
bathroom, there was water coming out the
bottom of the door, the sides of the door and
even the TOP of the door.

"Oh, dear," said Adam's father.

He opened the door really fast.

The whole bathroom was filled with water and Adam and his sister were swimming around inside.

Adam's father slammed the door before the water could get out.

He yelled, **"Adam! Pull the plug!"**

"Well," said Adam, "I might pull the plug if you got me a nice new skateboard."

So Adam's father went to the skateboard store and bought a nice new skateboard. Then he came back, opened the bathroom door really fast, threw in the skateboard before the water could get out, and slammed the door.

Then he yelled, **"Adam! Pull the plug!"**

"Well," said Adam, "I might pull the plug if you got me a new pair of red running shoes, and a new dress for my sister."

So Adam's father ran to the mall and bought Adam a pair of red running shoes, and a dress for his little sister. Then he came back, opened the bathroom door really fast, threw in the shoes and dress before the water could get out, and slammed the door.

Then he yelled,

## "Adam! Pull the plug!"

"Well," said Adam, "I might pull the plug if you got me an enormous hamburger."

So Adam's father drove to the hamburger store and bought an enormous hamburger for Adam. Then he came back, opened the bathroom door really fast, and threw in the hamburger before the water could get out.

Then he yelled really loud,

# "Adam! Pull the plug!"

So Adam swam down to the bottom
of the bathroom and pulled the plug in
the tub, and the water started to go
around and around and down the drain.

Swish! Swish! Swish! Swish! Swish!

Adam said, "My skateboard and
running shoes went down the drain!"

Swish! Swish! Swish! Swish! Swish!

Adam said, "My hamburger and my
dog went down the drain!"

Swish! Swish! Swish! Swish! Swish!

Adam said, "My sister and the cat
went down the drain!"

Swish! Swish! Swish! Swish! Swish!

"AHHHHHHHHHHHHHHHHH!" yelled Adam. "I'm going down the drain!"

"Oh, no!" said Adam's father. He opened up the bathroom door and there was . . .

No water!

No hamburger!

No shoes!

No skateboard!

No dog!

No cat!

No sister!

And . . . no Adam!

Adam's father called down the drain, "Adam! Are you okay?"

From way down the drain Adam said, "Yes."

His father said, "Adam! Climb out."

"I can't climb out," said Adam. "It's too far."

"Ride your skateboard," said his dad.

"It's too slippery," said Adam.

"Put on your new running shoes," said his dad.

"I'm too weak," said Adam.

"Eat your hamburger," said his dad.

So Adam put on his running shoes, ate his hamburger and got on his skateboard. In a minute he came up out of the drain, dragging everyone else behind him.

Adam looked at his father and said, "You have no idea what it is like down there. There is glitch, gloop, hair, old toenails, slop and glop. Look at me, I am covered with glitchy, gloopy, grimy GLOP!"

"YUCK!" yelled Adam's mom. She threw everyone into the tub, clothes and all.

And she called Grandma on her cell phone while everyone else had a bath.